11 12 13 14 15 16 17 18 19 20

31 32 33 34 35 36 37 38 39 40

51 52 53 54 55 56 5_ _ _ 60

71 72 73 74 75 76 77 78 79 80

91 92 93 94 95 96 97 98 99 100

111 112 113 114 115 116 117 118 119 120

31 132 133 134 135 136 137 138 139 140

151 152 153 154 155 156 157 158 159 160

171 172 173 174 175 176 177 178 179 180

191 192 193 194 195 196 197 198 199 200

211 212 213 214 215 216 217 218 219 220

231 232 233 234 235 236 237 238 239 240

251 252 253 254 255 256 257 258 259 260

271 272 273 274 275 276 277 278 279 280

291 292 293 294 295 296 297 298 299 300

1 2 3 4
5
6 7 8 9
10
11
12 13
4

Lauren Child

Absolutely ONE Thing

Featuring Charlie and Lola

CANDLEWICK PRESS

4 2sday For Tuesday

1

Copyright © 2015 by Lauren Child. Text design © 2015 by David Mackintosh.

First published in Great Britain in 2015 by Orchard Books.

First U.S. edition 2016.

This book was typeset in ITC Officina Serif.

Library of Congress Catalog Card Number 2015933254

ISBN 978-0-7636-8728-1

15 16 17 18 19 20 APS 10 9 8 7 6 5 4 3 2 1

Printed in Humen, Dongguan, China

Candlewick Press,
99 Dover Street,
Somerville,
Massachusetts 02144

visit us at www.candlewick.com

I have this little sister, Lola.
She is small and very funny.

Sometimes for a treat,
Mom says, "We are going to
the store and you may choose
one thing."

"One thing EACH," I say,
    "or ONE thing
        between TWO?"

And Mom says, "EACH."

I say to Lola,
"We are going to the store and we
are allowed to choose ONE thing."

"One thing to **share?**"
                        says Lola.

I say,
"One thing EACH,
which means TWO actual things."

            "**Two things?**" says Lola.

    "TWO things **between** TWO," I say.

Mom says we must be ready in TEN minutes.

It takes me **THREE** minutes to brush my teeth,

ONE minute to remember that

FOUR minutes

I have forgotten to eat breakfast,

to eat my puffa pops,

THREE minutes
to brush my teeth again

and
EIGHT minutes
to find Lola's

left
shoe.

Charlie

$$3 + 1 + 4 + 3 + 8 = 19$$

That makes us

NINE MINUTES LATE.

$$19 - 10 =$$

9 MINUTES LATE.

Lola shouts,
"I just need to do **something**."

I say,
"WHAT thing?"

She says,
"**One** thing."

I say,
"But we don't
have time…"

She says,
"I will be **half** of
a **second**."

after **TWO** whole minutes,

which is in fact

120 SECONDS,

This is **NOT** TRUE because

I go into our room to find Lola.

"What are you DOING?" I say.

Lola says,
"I am just trying to count the dots on my dress. But I am NOT sure what comes after twelve."

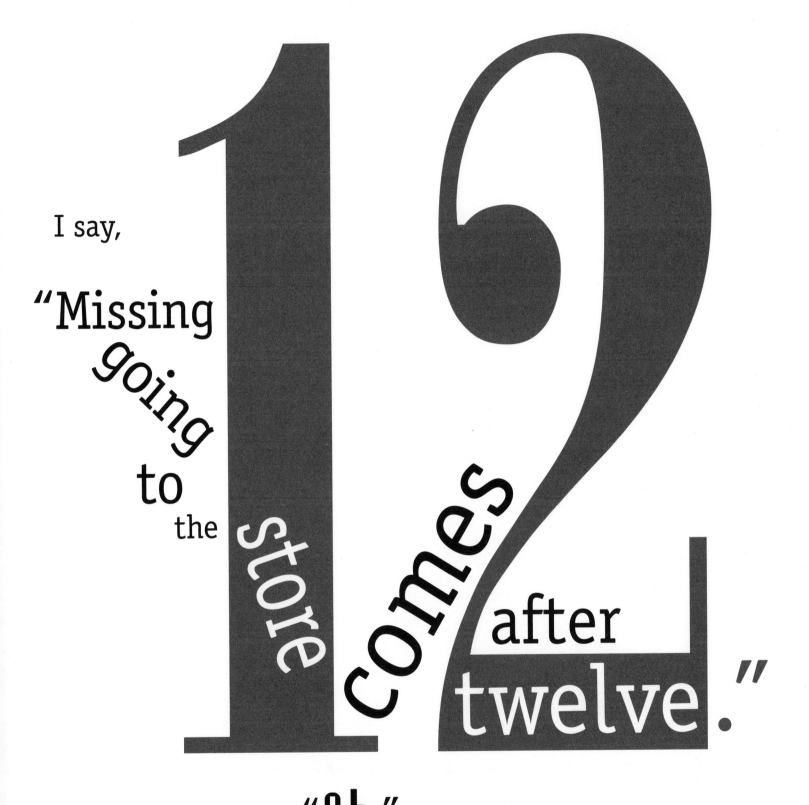

I say, "Missing going to the store comes after twelve."

"Oh," says Lola. "HURRY UP!"

I am running as fast as I can and Lola is counting ladybugs on the path.

She says,

"There are at least FIFTY or twenty-seventeen.

How **many** shoes would **FIFTY** or **twenty**-SEVENTEEN ladybugs **need**, Charlie?"

I say, "NONE, ladybugs DON'T WEAR SHOES."

"What about **socks**?" says Lola.

"No, they NEVER wear socks."

"It must be **very ouchy**," says Lola.

When we walk past the pond
we are followed by several ducks.

"How **many** ducks are **following** us?" asks Lola.

"THREE," I say.

Lola finds half a cookie in her coat pocket and starts feeding them crumbs.

"How many **now**?" she says.

I say, "THREE ducks, SEVEN pigeons, FIVE wading birds, FOUR swans, TWO geese, and ONE flapping bird."

$3 + 7 + 5 + 4 + 2 + 1 = 22$

"Run!"

shouts Lola.

Lola looks up at the sky and she says,
"Look at all of **those** singing birds—there are

one two five SEVEN twenty
sixteen eleventeen NINE birds singing."

are

1  2

there

"NO, Lola,

And I say,

"That's
what I **said**,"
she says.

"I said **nine**."

I say,
"Well, if you are
so good at counting,
then how many **leaves**
are there on that tree?"

"A **hundred**," says Lola,
"nearly at **least**."

I say,
"There are
MORE THAN
a **hundred**,
more than
A THOUSAND,
even."

"How many is a **thousand**?" says Lola.

"TEN HUNDREDS make A THOUSAND," I say.

$$10 \times 100 = 1000$$

"And is a **thousand** the **most**?" says Lola.

I say, "No, then there is a MILLION and that is

"And is a **million** MORE than the **rain**?" says Lola.

"or **maybe** even a TRILLION."

"Or a

squil

a THOUSAND times **more**."

"No, the rain is probably a **billion**," I say,

lion?"

says Lola.

I say,
"I don't know if a
SQUILLION is a **number**."

When we
get there,
Mom says,
"You
may
choose
one
thing."

And Lola says,

"**Three** things."

3

steps to walk to the store.

156

And Mom says,
"ONE thing."

1

And Lola says,
"**Two** things."

2

And Mom says,
"How about NO things?"

And Lola says,
"How
about
one
thing?"

And Mom says,
"Absolutely ONE thing."

And Lola says,

"Yes, **one** thing."

I spend THREE minutes looking at the comics
and TWO minutes looking at the pins and
I make up my mind in FIVE seconds.

I choose the
SIX pins.

Lola is still looking.

After ELEVEN minutes, Mom says,
"Hurry up, Lola, we are leaving in
one minute."

TWO minutes
later, Lola
chooses twelve
stickers.

On the way home, Lola sticks FIVE stickers on the pavement, THREE on a tree, TWO on her shoes, and ONE on me. She even sticks ONE on Marv's dog.

By the time we get home there are NO stickers left. NONE.

12 - 5 - 3 - 2 - 1 - 1 = 0

We have been home for FOUR minutes when Lola says, "**please** can I have **One** of your **pins**, Charlie?"

And I say, "OK, you can have ONE." 1

She says, "Maybe **perhaps** even **three**?"

And I say, 3 1 "ONE."

And she says, "Or **two**?" 2

And I say, "How about NONE?" 0

And
she says,

"OK, yes
please, one."

1	2	3	4	5	6	7	8	9	10
21	22	23	24	25	26	27	28	29	30
41	42	43	44	45	46	47	48	49	50
61	62	63	64	65	66	67	68	69	70
81	82	83	84	85	86	87	88	89	90
101	102	103	104	105	106	107	108	109	110
121	122	123	124	125	126	127	128	129	130
141	142	143	144	145	146	147	148	149	150
161	162	163	164	165	166	167	168	169	170
181	182	183	184	185	186	187	188	189	190
201	202	203	204	205	206	207	208	209	210
221	222	223	224	225	226	227	228	229	230
241	242	243	245	245	246	247	248	249	250
261	262	263	264	265	266	267	268	269	270
281	282	283	284	285	286	287	288	289	290